ANNUAL 2011

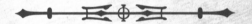

MERLIN: THE OFFICIAL ANNUAL 2011
A BANTAM BOOK 978 0 553 82214 4

First published in Great Britain by Bantam,
an imprint of Random House Children's Books
A Random House Group Company.

This edition published 2010

1 3 5 7 9 10 8 6 4 2

Text copyright © Bantam, 2010
© 2010 Shine Limited. Licensed by FremantleMedia Enterprises.
Merlin created by Julian Jones, Jake Michie, Julian Murphy and Johnny Capps.

Bantam Books are published by Random House Children's Books,
61–63 Uxbridge Road, London W5 5SA

www.rbooks.co.uk
www.kidsatrandomhouse.co.uk

Addresses for companies within The Random House Group Limited can be found at:
www.randomhouse.co.uk/offices.htm

THE RANDOM HOUSE GROUP Limited Reg. No. 954009

A CIP catalogue record for this book is available from the British Library

Printed in Italy

CONTENTS

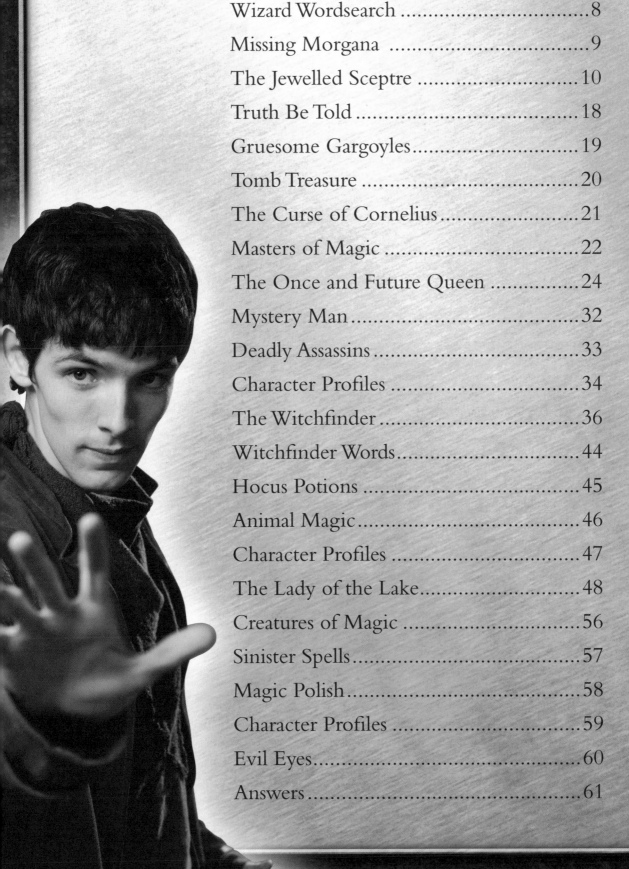

MERLIN

Merlin is destined to become a great warlock, but he cannot yet reveal his magic in Camelot. As long as sorcery is outlawed in Uther's kingdom, this gentle but courageous young man must remain just a humble manservant to the prince. Merlin's destiny is to keep Arthur from harm and ensure that one day he becomes a great king . . . which means hardly a day goes by when Merlin doesn't have to come to his rescue.

ARTHUR

As heir to the throne, Prince Arthur has the future of Camelot on his shoulders. Although he is a brave and skilful knight, enemies of the Pendragons are growing in number and he is constantly under threat. Whilst he outwardly treats Merlin as he would any other servant, the increasingly strong bond between the two means they would stop at nothing to protect one another.

MORGANA

Morgana has always suffered from strange and vivid nightmares, but they are growing in intensity and she is beginning to suspect they are a symptom of what sets her apart from everyone else: magic. Through fear of rejection from Uther, she has begun to seek counsel from sources outside Camelot. Although Merlin longs to help, he cannot risk his life by revealing that he is himself a warlock.

GWEN

Guinevere is not simply the gentle maidservant that she appears. She is fiercely loyal to her mistress, Morgana, and counts her as a close friend. Although she has strong feelings for Arthur – feelings that he returns – she is not afraid to stand up to him and tell him what she thinks. She believes that her humble background makes a relationship with the prince impossible . . . but could Arthur change the rules once he becomes king?

WIZARD WORDSEARCH

Look carefully at this wordsearch square and see if you can find all the Merlin words and characters listed. The words read up, down, backwards, forwards and diagonally.

D	R	A	G	O	N	L	O	R	D	H	T	O	S
E	B	X	Z	M	T	O	L	E	C	N	A	L	J
R	U	H	T	R	A	H	A	L	I	G	B	N	U
D	R	A	G	O	N	N	S	C	Q	V	A	A	T
R	Y	L	A	R	E	D	I	A	N	Y	L	I	H
O	D	I	N	W	M	R	G	T	E	S	I	V	E
M	O	R	G	A	N	A	K	R	J	A	N	I	R
O	E	T	B	D	W	Y	F	I	P	N	O	V	S
R	R	R	A	V	L	A	C	N	R	O	R	Y	M
G	X	O	L	W	S	U	I	A	G	J	T	C	S
A	P	L	L	I	H	T	R	I	C	K	L	E	R
U	Q	L	N	A	N	B	D	D	E	N	I	L	A
S	I	G	A	N	F	H	E	N	G	I	S	T	M
E	T	O	L	E	M	A	C	U	R	S	E	K	L

CAMELOT	DRAGON	LANCELOT	VIVIAN
UTHER	CEDRIC	ALVARR	AREDIAN
ARTHUR	SIGAN	ALINED	MORGAUSE
MERLIN	CURSE	CATRINA	FREYA
MORGANA	MYROR	TROLL	HALIG
GWEN	ODIN	JONAS	BALINOR
GAIUS	MORDRED	OLAF	DRAGONLORD
	HENGIST	TRICKLER	

MISSING MORGANA

Morgana is at the Druid camp in the Forest of Ascetir and her disappearance
has caused panic in Camelot. Which way should Merlin go to find her?
Watch out for deadly Serkets along the way!

THE JEWELLED SCEPTRE

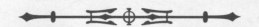

The jewelled sceptre on the newly opened tomb looked like a wonderful prize, but the workman who found it had died horribly. That didn't deter crafty thief Cedric, though. He wanted that gem, and he was going to get it! When he found out Prince Arthur had the keys to the burial chamber, he came up with a sly plan – he would become the prince's servant! Then he would be able to get hold of the keys and enter the locked chamber. Of course, Arthur already had a servant: Merlin. But Cedric wasn't going to let that stop him . . .

Cedric accompanied Arthur on a hunting expedition. During the hunt, a boar charged the prince and would have killed him if Merlin hadn't used magic to throw a spear at the beast. But Cedric claimed responsibility for saving Arthur. 'I shall be for ever indebted to you,' Arthur told him. 'You must be rewarded.'

'I desire but one thing, sire,' said Cedric. 'A position in the royal household.'

Of course, Merlin didn't protest because he couldn't admit to casting a spell! The next day, he was horrified to find that Cedric had taken over his duties and was attending to Prince Arthur. And worse still, Arthur seemed to think Cedric was a much better servant than Merlin. 'Although I regret, sire, there is one thing I've failed to do,' Cedric told the prince. 'Muck out your horses . . .'

Merlin reluctantly started the dirty job. Sneaky Cedric followed him and tossed a knock-out smoke bomb into the stables. Merlin fell asleep and Cedric released all the horses. There was chaos in the lower town as the animals ran amok! Arthur decided that as Merlin had made such a mess of things, Cedric should take over as the prince's servant that night. This was just the opportunity Cedric had been waiting for. When Arthur went to bed, Cedric stole his keys and made straight for the tomb.

The glowing blue gem in the sceptre seemed to call to him, and he hurriedly prised the heart-shaped jewel from its clasp. Suddenly, a strange blue-white gas seeped out of the stone and entered his mouth, nose and ears. The tomb belonged to an ancient sorcerer, Cornelius Sigan, who had encased his soul within the gem. Now Cedric had removed the jewel, Sigan was able to take over his body and live again!

Gaius found the discarded gem and realized what had happened. 'Sigan swore that he would one day return and raze Camelot to the ground,' he warned. Merlin then tried to tell Arthur that Cedric had been possessed by the spirit of Sigan, but the prince wouldn't believe him. 'Merlin, this nonsense isn't helping you keep your job,' he said.

'I don't care about my job!' said Merlin, frustrated.

Arthur wasn't amused. 'If that's what you feel, it makes my task a lot easier,' he replied. He ordered Cedric to escort Merlin from the palace, but the warlock resisted – and got locked in the cells for his pains.

Meanwhile, Sigan was planning a terrible fate for all of Camelot. 'The earth will roar, the sky will burn and these very walls shall dance to my command,' he bellowed. 'You will tremble before my vengeance and you shall pray to me for mercy. But you shall know none.'

He cast a
powerful spell
and the castle's
winged-monkey
gargoyles came
to life! They
attacked the
people of Camelot,
causing panic
throughout the
city. Arthur and his
knights tried to fight back, but their weapons were no match for
the magical creatures and the prince was
seriously wounded. However, he
refused to rest. 'Some of the
townspeople are trapped on
the drawbridge,' he told
Uther. 'I will not leave
them to die.'

'Arthur, no, this is suicide!'
cried his father, but the
prince took no notice. He
had to rescue his people.
With his knights, he raced off
to confront the monsters.

Then the castle of Camelot itself began to crack and crumble! Down in the dungeons, Merlin could hear the panic above. He knew he had to help Arthur. With a single spell, he broke out of his cell. There was only one place he could go for advice – to the Great Dragon. Merlin had sworn never to visit the Dragon again, but he would have to swallow his pride if Arthur and the kingdom were to be saved.

The Dragon told Merlin he would need a powerful spell of the Old Religion to defeat Sigan, and he would give it to Merlin – but only if the young sorcerer offered him something in return. 'What?' asked the warlock, worried.

'A promise that one day you will free me,' said the Dragon. 'You must promise, or Camelot will fall.'

Merlin didn't trust the Dragon, but he had no choice. He had to promise.

Arthur and his knights attacked the winged monkeys, but during the fight the prince got separated from his men. The knights made it back to the palace. Arthur had almost joined them when a gargoyle dived at him. 'Save yourselves!' Arthur yelled. Reluctantly, the knights shut the doors so the creature couldn't get at the king. The prince was trapped outside, alone.

'Where's Arthur?' cried King Uther in a panic, realizing his son wasn't with the rest of the knights. He wanted to open the doors, but one of the knights held him back, knowing they would all die if the gargoyles got into the palace. Just then the room began to collapse around them and they had to run for safety.

Arthur's wounds proved too much for him and he fell to the ground, unconscious. A winged monkey swooped down towards him, going for the kill. The prince didn't stand a chance. But then there was a flash of light, and the creature turned back to stone in mid air. It fell to the ground and shattered into a thousand pieces. Merlin emerged from the shadows. It was his magic that had defeated the monster!

The warlock hurried over to Arthur, but Sigan – in Cedric's body – arrived at the same time. 'Who would have believed it?' Sigan said. 'You, a sorcerer. And a powerful one.'

'I won't let you hurt him,' said Merlin.

Sigan tried to turn Merlin against Arthur, reminding the boy how badly the prince had treated him. 'He does not deserve your loyalty. He treats you like a slave,' the ancient sorcerer said. Sigan even tried to bribe Merlin. 'You have yet to discover your true power. I can help you. Together we can rule over this land. Arthur will tremble at your voice. He will kneel at your feet.'

But Merlin didn't want that. 'Better to serve a good man than to rule with an evil one,' he declared.

'So be it,' said Sigan. 'If you won't join me, I will become you and your power shall be harnessed to my will. The walls of Camelot will crumble and all who dwell within shall be destroyed.' A mist came out of Cedric's mouth and crept towards Merlin – Sigan was going to take over Merlin's body!

But Merlin had the Dragon's powerful spell. With a tremendous effort, he fought off the sorcerer and trapped his soul back in the heart-shaped gem.

Camelot was safe. Merlin knew he wouldn't get any thanks for his efforts – no one except Gaius could know that he'd used magic. But then Arthur turned up to visit and, to Merlin's amazement, the prince admitted Merlin had been right about Cedric. Arthur claimed he wasn't really apologizing though – he just wanted Merlin to return to his service because his armour needed cleaning!

TRUTH BE TOLD

How much do you remember about Merlin's adventure?
Say whether these statements are **TRUE** or **FALSE** and then check
your answers to see how much attention you were paying!

		TRUE	FALSE
1.	Merlin's magic saved Arthur from a charging bull.		☒
2.	Merlin let out Arthur's horses.		☒
3.	Cedric stole the key to the tomb while Arthur was asleep.	☒	
4.	The tomb's heart-shaped jewel glowed green.		
5.	Sigan's powerful spell brought the castle's gargoyles to life.		
6.	Merlin stole keys from the guards to get out of his cell.		
7.	The Great Dragon agreed to help, but only if Merlin promised to free him.		
8.	Merlin used magic to save Arthur from a gargoyle attack.		
9.	Sigan convinced Merlin that Arthur treated him badly.		
10.	Sigan's soul took control of Merlin's body.		

GRUESOME GARGOYLES

All kinds of strange stone sculptures were dotted around Camelot to ward off evil spirits – that's why they were so ugly! Do your worst here and draw the scariest gargoyle ever.

TOMB TREASURE

The cursed tomb of Cornelius Sigan held all kinds of precious treasures. See if you can complete the mysterious number sequences on these gold plates!

3	6	9	12	15	18
1	2	4	7	11	16
5	9	13	17	21	25
16	13	10	7	4	1
4	8	12	16	20	24
2	9	16	23	30	37

THE CURSE OF CORNELIUS

How many words can you make from the letters in 'Cornelius'? You can use each letter no more than once for each word. The first one is done for you – it's 'curse', of course! See if you can make twenty in all. If you get stuck, have a peek at page 61.

CORNELIUS

1. curse
2. corn
3. rinse
4. run
5. cone
6. lie
7. sun
8. con
9. relic
10. ore
11. is
12. us
13. one
14. urn
15. lion
16. sole
17. slur
18. rice
19. nice
20. lone

MASTERS OF MAGIC

Do you know if a Serket should be slain or stroked?

Was Aredian feared or revered?

Do this quiz on Merlin's latest adventures to see if you're a scholar of sorcery or mystified by magic! Check your answers with those at the bottom of the page and give yourself a point for each correct one to get your score.

1. The Serkets that attacked Morgana in the Forest of Ascetir were what sort of creature?

a) Giant maggots

b) Giant scorpions

c) Giant rats

2. What did Lady Catrina give to Uther as a gift?

a) An enchanted pendant

b) A silver goblet

c) A lock of her hair

3. Which ruler sent an assassin to kill Arthur?

a) Olaf

b) Cenred

c) Odin

4. Aredian was renowned for being what?

a) A Witchfinder

b) A Goldsmith

c) A Scrivener

5. How was Morgause related to Morgana?

a) She was her aunt

b) She was her half-sister

c) She was her cousin

6. Who had the only key to Cornelius Sigan's tomb?

a) Arthur

b) Uther

c) Morgana

7. What weapon was used in the first round of Olaf's challenge to Arthur?

a) The quarterstaff

b) The broadsword

c) The lance

8. Merlin used magic to bring what down on Halig's head?

a) An anvil

b) A wheelbarrow

c) A tavern sign

9. To whose kingdom did Merlin and Arthur go in search of the last Dragonlord?

a) Cenred's

b) Alined's

c) Odin's

10. How many Knights of Medhir did Morgause bring to life?

a) Five

b) Seven

c) Nine

11. Which vicious beasts did Hengist keep for entertainment?

a) Griffins

b) Dragons

c) Wilddeoren

12. Which magical artefact did Alvarr want?

a) The Star of Camelot

b) The Ring of Aquitaine

c) The Crystal of Neahtid

How did you score?

10 or more: Not much gets past you – you're without doubt a master of magic!

5–9: Pretty good, but you're still at apprentice level. Practice makes perfect, though!

4 or less: You're bewildered by bewitchment, but don't give up. It'll make sense eventually!

Answers: 1.b 2.a 3.c 4.a 5.b 6.a 7.a
8.c 9.a 10.b 11.c 12.c

THE ONCE AND FUTURE QUEEN

Prince Arthur was the winner!

Of course, Prince Arthur was always the winner.

But this time, he should have lost. Arthur and his knights were practising jousting, riding at each other with lances. Sunlight glaring off his opponent's armour had made Arthur blink and Sir Leon should have been able to knock the prince off his horse – but instead, the knight swerved away.

'Why did you pull out?' Arthur demanded angrily. 'You can't afford to hesitate.'

'I wouldn't if I were facing a different opponent,' Sir Leon said. 'You are the future king, my lord.'

Arthur realized with horror that his knights weren't trying their best when they fought him – they were too scared of beating the Crown Prince of Camelot. None of his victories meant anything.

'All my life I've been treated as if I'm something special,' he told Merlin later. 'I just want to be treated like everyone else.'

Soon the prince came up with a plan. He would compete in the forthcoming jousting tournament – but in disguise! Then he'd know for sure if he could win through his own merits.

Arthur told his father that he was leaving Camelot for a while. Then he went to Gwen's house, where he planned to stay out of sight until the tournament was over.

Arthur could joust in the tournament as his face would be covered by a helmet, but there were also the matters of greeting the crowd and being presented to the king. He needed a stand-in. Merlin recruited a farmer called William, who wasn't known to anyone in Camelot. After the competition, Arthur would reveal his true identity.

Gwen wasn't enjoying having Arthur to stay. He took the only bed in the house, and expected her to wait on him. He might say he wanted to be treated like anyone else, but he didn't act like it. She couldn't wait for the tournament to be over, so her house guest could return to his own bed in the palace.

Meanwhile, King Uther had received some worrying news. Odin, ruler of a neighbouring kingdom, had sent an assassin to Camelot to kill Prince Arthur. The king was relieved that Arthur was away from the city, not realizing that he was really very close at hand – and that the assassin, Myror, was already scouting out the area, trying to discover where Arthur might be hiding.

Arthur, disguised as 'Sir William of Deira', was winning all his bouts in the tournament. The only person not cheering for him was Gwen. 'I believe he's an arrogant pig,' she told Gaius.

At last only Sir William and Sir Alynor remained in the competition.

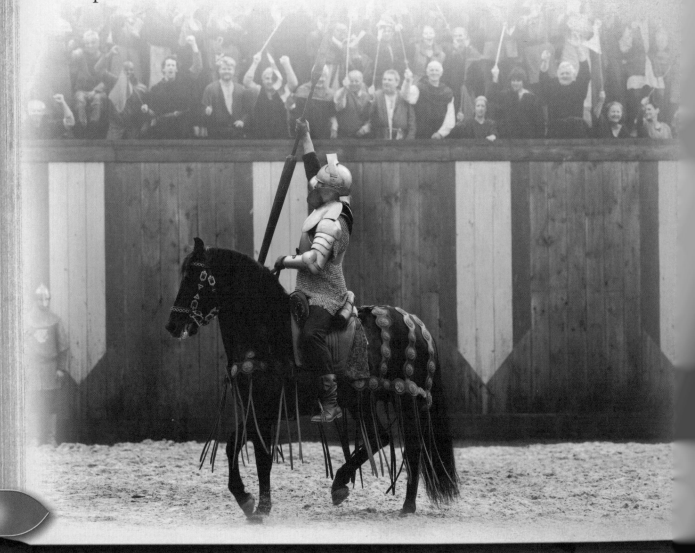

Merlin was looking after Arthur's horse when a stranger came up to him. 'So, you're no longer working for Prince Arthur?' the stranger said.

Merlin wasn't sure what to say. 'No . . . Yes . . . Not right now. Arthur's away,' he told the man.

The stranger wished him farewell and moved off. Merlin went back to his duties. He didn't realize that he'd just been talking to the assassin – and his confused answer had given the man a big clue as to how he might find Arthur.

Arthur returned to Gwen's house. She hadn't been expecting him so soon, and wasn't in time to hide her makeshift bed on the stone floor.

The prince was horrified. He hadn't realized that he'd taken Gwen's bed. He began to see that he'd acted thoughtlessly and selfishly. It was obvious that Gwen was angry with him, and he asked her why. 'You claim titles don't matter to you, but you behave like a prince and expect me to wait on you like a servant,' she said. 'Would it kill you to say please and thank you once in a while?'

No one had ever spoken to Arthur like that before. He knew that her words were true, and he felt ashamed. 'You're right,' he told her. 'You have invited me into your home and I have behaved appallingly. I'll make it up to you. I'll make dinner for you tonight.'

Gwen was amazed and pleased. But when she'd left to go for a walk, Arthur realized that he didn't have the faintest idea how to cook. Luckily, just then Merlin arrived. 'I need you to fetch me two dinners from the palace kitchens,' Arthur said. 'But don't tell Gwen.'

Myror the assassin had been following Merlin. Keeping track of the prince's servant seemed a good way to find the prince. He watched the boy bring two plates of food from the palace kitchens to a small house in the town. Shortly afterwards, the boy left and a pretty girl entered the house.

Myror crept up to the window. There was Prince Arthur himself, sitting at a table with the girl! Myror aimed a small crossbow at Arthur and was about to fire when a guard patrol came along. He'd been spotted! The assassin made a hurried getaway.

Arthur was pleased to see how much Gwen enjoyed their meal together. Her outburst had cleared the air, and they were happy and comfortable in each other's presence. It was strange, Arthur thought, that he'd enjoyed this small dinner in these humble surroundings much more than any vast banquet he'd had in the palace. It must be the company . . .

But then disaster struck. Gwen noticed that the plates they'd been eating from had the royal seal on them! She realized that he hadn't really cooked a meal for her at all.

Arthur sighed. 'Look, I can kill a chicken from

a thousand paces, just don't ask me to cook it. That's what servants are for.'

He realized as he said it that he'd insulted her again.

'I'm not ashamed to be a servant,' she told him. 'A good king should respect his people no matter who they are.'

'I know I have much to learn,' he said. 'There are some things that I'm terrible at – cooking being one of them – but also, knowing what to say to someone I care about . . .' Because he'd realized that he did care for Gwen, a lot.

He might have said more – but just then Merlin burst through the door. He'd run all the way from the palace, where he'd heard some worrying news from Gaius. 'There's an assassin in Camelot!' Merlin cried. 'He's here to kill Arthur!'

Arthur told Merlin and Gwen that Odin's son had challenged him to a fight. Arthur had tried to get the boy to withdraw, but he wouldn't. They had fought, and to the prince's great sorrow, the boy had been killed. He wasn't surprised to learn that Odin wanted revenge.

At least the assassin wouldn't know where to find Arthur, Merlin commented. But the assassin knew more than Merlin suspected, and was already making plans . . .

The next morning, Arthur was preparing for the final. 'You can go back to being Prince Arthur soon,' Gwen said. She handed him a neckerchief. 'I thought you might wear it for luck.'

Arthur took it. 'Thank you,' he said. He realized just how much he was going to miss being close to Gwen. Before he knew quite what he was doing, he leaned forward and kissed her.

For a moment, their lips met. Then, confused, Arthur broke away. 'I must go,' he said, and hurried off.

Myror killed Sir Alynor, and dressed himself in the knight's armour. No one would realize he was an impostor. He had a lance that was specially rigged to shoot out a sharp spike as he neared Arthur in combat. By the time anyone worked out what had happened, it would be too late.

But Myror reckoned without Merlin and his magical vision. Watching the tournament, the warlock saw Arthur being stabbed. He followed Alynor and discovered that he was really the assassin!

Meanwhile, Gwen was tending to Arthur's wounds. To her dismay, he wanted to continue with the fight, despite being badly hurt. He went back out on the field, and Merlin arrived too late with his warning. There was only one thing to do. As the assassin

rode towards Arthur, Merlin cast a spell that broke his saddle. The prince was easily able to unhorse his distracted opponent. Myror fell badly, and was killed. The danger was over.

'Time to reveal yourself to the crowd,' Merlin told Arthur. But Arthur, looking at Gwen, told William the farmer to claim the prize instead. 'Perhaps this is a time for humility,' he said, and she smiled.

Arthur persuaded King Uther not to strike back at Odin. 'There's been enough bloodshed,' he said. He saw that Gwen, watching from the side of the council chamber, looked pleased and proud at his words. But he had something very difficult to say to her.

Arthur waited for her outside. 'What happened while I was staying with you,' he began. 'I'm afraid my father would never understand,' he finished slowly.

Gwen lost her smile. 'You don't have to explain,' she said. 'Perhaps things will be different when you're king.'

Watching her walk off, wondering about what he'd just said goodbye to, Prince Arthur hoped she was right.

MYSTERY MAN

Look carefully at these two pictures of the talented newcomer
'Sir William of Deira'. Can you spot the ten differences between them?

DEADLY ASSASSINS

Myror is just one of the would-be assassins that have tried to kill Arthur. Unjumble the letters to find six other murderous menaces that Merlin has saved the prince from!

1. lakgofin

_ _ _ _ _ _ _ _

2. slinarlomyc

_ _ _ _ _ _ _ _ _ _ _

3. cradylatani

_ _ _ _ _ _ _ _ _ _ _

4. knaan

_ _ _ _ _

5. terrogadang

_ _ _ _ _ _ _ _ _ _ _ _

6. tailkingthanv

_ _ _ _ _ _ _ _ _ _ _ _ _

GAIUS

Gaius, the court physician, is the only person in Camelot who knows about Merlin's magical powers and is himself a former sorcerer. Whenever Merlin feels burdened by his gift, this wise old mentor is always there to offer support. Knowing the importance of the young warlock's role in Arthur's destiny, Gaius is so loyal that he has, on more than one occasion, offered his own life to save Merlin's.

UTHER

King Uther's aim is to be a just ruler, but his war on magic and all who practise it has often been brutal. He would punish any member of his household thought to be involved in sorcery. As a stern and demanding parent, he shows his love for Arthur by pushing him hard to achieve his potential, and able as he is, Arthur constantly strives for his father's approval.

LANCELOT

Having abandoned his impossible dream of becoming a Knight of Camelot, Lancelot now survives by prizefighting. Gwen met him again when she was imprisoned in Hengist's castle and he was entertaining the bandit crowds. His legendary courage and deep feelings for Gwen were proven once again when he risked his life to help her escape.

THE GREAT DRAGON

The only Dragon that survived Uther's purge of magic was imprisoned deep beneath Camelot. Merlin often asked his advice, but the Great Dragon's help came at a price: freedom. When Merlin released him, Kilgarrah unleashed a deadly attack. Merlin confronted him, but spared the beast's life on the condition he never return. Humbled, the Great Dragon agreed but, just before leaving, declared that their paths would cross again . . .

BALINOR

Forced into hiding by the Great Purge, Balinor spent twenty years as a hermit in the wild. As the last Dragonlord, he was the only person left with the power to communicate with the Great Dragon. It was only when his help was needed in Camelot that Merlin discovered the truth: the exceptional warlock who held the key to the future of the kingdom was his father.

THE WITCHFINDER

Sometimes being Prince Arthur's servant was no fun at all. Merlin was really tired from doing so much boring work like fixing the prince's armour and scrubbing his chambers. One day, when he was out in the woods collecting logs, he sat down and cast a spell to cheer himself up. He made the smoke from a fire turn into the shape of a horse.

But someone saw the smoky stallion! A villager had been walking in the woods, and ran off to tell King Uther she had witnessed sorcery! To Merlin's horror, the king immediately announced that he would send for the Witchfinder, a man whose hatred of magic was seemingly as great as Uther's own.

The Witchfinder, Aredian, had harsh words for Uther when he arrived. 'The stench of sorcery infects Camelot like a contagion,' he said. 'You have grown lazy and idle – you stand on the brink of dark oblivion.' The king agreed to pay Aredian any price he asked in return for his help in ridding the city of magic.

Aredian summoned Merlin to his chambers to ask questions about the mystical horse. Merlin denied everything, but the Witchfinder didn't believe him.

The whole court assembled in the throne room. Aredian produced three female witnesses who claimed to have seen strange magic – screaming faces, dancing goblins and a sorcerer with toads coming out of his mouth. He announced that the sorcerer was in the room. Everyone was alarmed – especially Morgana, who feared that her secret was about to be revealed. But the Witchfinder pointed his finger at Merlin.

'You can't be serious!' cried Arthur.

'This is outrageous! You have no evidence!' Gaius said angrily.

The king agreed that Aredian could search Merlin's room to find proof. He and Uther's guards turned Gaius' chambers upside down. To the physician's surprise – and horror – they found a magical amulet. Desperately trying to protect Merlin, Gaius claimed it belonged to him, and was dragged off to the dungeons.

'Gaius has served me with unfailing dedication. He turned his back on sorcery,' Uther told the Witchfinder. But Aredian persuaded the king to let him interrogate Gaius – just to make sure.

Gaius bravely refused to confess to using magic, but accidentally revealed that he was treating Morgana for nightmares. The Witchfinder pounced on his words and immediately started to investigate.

'Well, Gaius, are you prepared to confess?' he demanded the next morning.

'I'd rather die,' answered Gaius defiantly.

The Witchfinder smiled. 'And die you shall. But not alone, I'm pleased to say. Merlin and the Lady Morgana are to join you in the flames – unless you admit your guilt.'

Gaius felt he had no choice but to agree to what Aredian asked. He was dragged in front of Uther. 'I am a sorcerer, sire,' he told the king, and claimed responsibility for all the magic that had been seen in Camelot. Merlin watched in horror as Uther sentenced the physician to death.

Arthur took Merlin to see Gaius in the cells. 'I can't believe Uther could do this to you,' Merlin said.

'He had no choice,' Gaius told him bravely. 'Once Aredian found the amulet . . .'

Gaius said he'd admitted owning the amulet in order to protect Merlin. 'But it's not mine!' the boy announced. He suddenly realized what had happened. Aredian must have planted it! 'If I can prove it, you're saved!' he told Gaius.

But the physician refused to let him try. 'Aredian will trap you into incriminating yourself,' he told the boy. 'It's suicide to investigate.' Merlin was very unhappy as he left the cell.

Gaius was very unhappy too. But at least Merlin and Morgana should be safe, he reflected. His confession meant that the Witchfinder's job was done.

He was horrified to discover that he was wrong. 'I thought you'd want to hear the news,' Aredian told him later. 'My investigations have begun.'

'Begun?' cried Gaius. 'But I've already confessed!'

'Indeed. Which just leaves Merlin and Morgana.'

Gaius stared at him in alarm. 'But we struck a bargain!'

'I don't bargain with sorcerers,' said the Witchfinder.

Merlin told Gwen that Aredian had planted the amulet in Gaius' chambers. 'But why would he do such a thing?' she asked.

Merlin had a theory. 'He's paid to catch sorcerers. Maybe he doesn't care whether someone is guilty or not. As long as he gets a confession, he gets his money.'

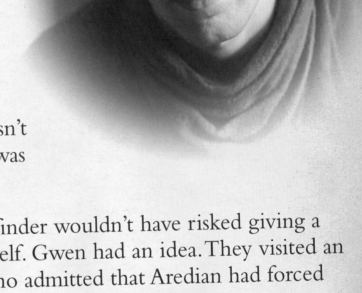

Despite Gaius' pleas, Merlin was determined to prove the physician's innocence. He sneaked into the Witchfinder's chambers and discovered some belladonna flowers in a cupboard. A tincture made from belladonna can cause hallucinations. 'Aredian's witnesses – it wasn't magic they were seeing, it was visions!' Merlin realized.

He guessed that the Witchfinder wouldn't have risked giving a potion to the women himself. Gwen had an idea. They visited an apothecary in the town, who admitted that Aredian had forced him to sell eye-drops containing belladonna.

Merlin wanted to rush straight to Uther. But Gwen realized that even though they now had evidence, the king would never believe the word of two servants above that of a trusted ally. 'We have to give Uther something he cannot deny, something not even Aredian can talk his way out of,' she insisted.

Merlin realized what he had to do. His magic had got them into this mess in the first place – now it would have to get them out of it. But he had to work fast, as Gaius was going to be burned at the stake the very next morning.

That night he crept into Aredian's chambers, made his way to the cupboard where he'd found the flowers, and cast a spell . . . Now they just had to keep Gaius alive until they could convince Uther of the Witchfinder's guilt.

In the morning, Gaius was dragged to the stake. Gwen desperately ran up to Arthur. 'You've got to stop this!' she told him. 'Merlin has proof that Gaius is innocent!'

Aredian grabbed a torch and thrust it into the bonfire built around Gaius' feet. 'Wait!' Arthur cried.

Gwen breathed a sigh of relief. Gaius was safe – but for how long?

Nervously, the apothecary stood before the king and admitted that Aredian had forced him to sell belladonna to the women who later claimed to have seen magic. Of course, the Witchfinder denied everything. 'Merlin has concocted these lies in the hope of saving his master,' he told Uther.

It looked like the king was going to believe Aredian, but Arthur requested that they search the Witchfinder's chambers for proof. Aredian did not object – until Arthur opened the cupboard in his room and revealed it to be full of potions and amulets!

'This is a trick!' Aredian cried, starting to cough. As Uther watched, Aredian choked even harder, and a toad leaped from his mouth!

Arthur reached for his sword, but the Witchfinder was too quick. He seized Morgana and put a blade to her throat. Merlin acted at once. As all eyes were on Aredian, the young warlock risked casting another spell. The handle of Aredian's sword glowed red hot, and he dropped it with a scream of pain. The Witchfinder stumbled backwards . . . and fell through the window, plummeting to his doom in the castle courtyard far below.

The next day, Gaius, free once more, tried to repair the damage Aredian had done to his chambers. Uther came to see him. 'I can scarcely believe Aredian was a sorcerer,' the king said. 'I wanted to say I'm sorry if you suffered at his hands.'

'But I didn't suffer at his hands,' Gaius replied. 'I suffered at yours. You see foes where there are friends. You see sorcerers where there are but servants. I am not the first to have been wrongly accused in your war against magic. And not all have been as lucky as I.'

Uther was astonished to be spoken to so bluntly – but he could not deny the truth of Gaius' words. For perhaps the first time ever, the king felt ashamed.

'There's one thing I don't understand,' Gaius said later to Merlin. 'How did you know he'd concealed evidence in his chamber?'

'Just a hunch,' Merlin replied evasively. He wasn't going to tell Gaius he'd used magic to fill the cupboard!

'And the toad?'

'That, er, I can't explain,' said the warlock.

Gaius looked stern. 'I can hardly explain it myself – unless, of course, you put it there.'

Merlin gave in. 'OK, Gaius, fair enough, I promise I will never save your life again.'

'You promise?' said Gaius.

'Absolutely.' They both laughed. Merlin had played the Witchfinder at his own game – and beaten him.

WITCHFINDER WORDS

See if you can solve these clues and complete the crossword
without looking back at the story!

ACROSS

3. The animal shape that Merlin
   conjured from smoke *(5)*

5. A villager ran to tell this person
   what she had seen *(5)*

6. The magic object found in
   Gaius' chambers *(6)*

7. The flower extract that caused
   hallucinations *(10)*

9. Gaius treated her for nightmares *(7)*

10. A medieval chemist *(10)*

12. Merlin used magic to make this
    too hot to handle *(5)*

DOWN

1. Gaius' role in the royal household *(9)*

2. The Witchfinder summoned
   by Uther *(7)*

4. A wooden post used to burn
   sorcerers on *(5)*

8. An underground prison *(7)*

11. A warty amphibian that comes
    from the mouths of sorcerers *(4)*

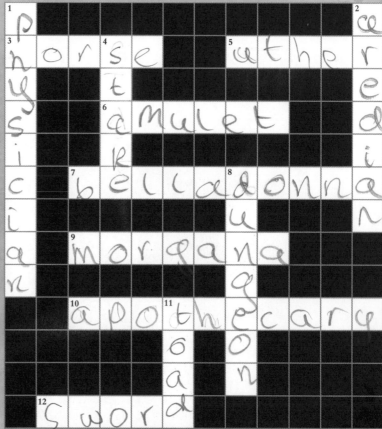

Across/Down solutions filled in:
1. physician
2. aredian
3. horse
5. uther
6. amulet
7. belladonna
9. morgana
10. apothecary
12. sword

HOCUS POTIONS

Aredian had more than belladonna in his bag of tricks!

Use the key to work out what other nasty potions the Witchfinder used to make people think they were seeing magic.

ᚠᛒᛁᛩᛗᛘᚷᚸᚺᛁᛂᛏᛚ

a b c d e f g h i j k l

ᛘᚾᛆᚠᚲᚱᛋᛏᚢᛈᚹᛃᛊ

m n o p r s t u w x y z

1 wolfsbane

2 hemlock

3 mandrake

4 mugwort

ANIMAL MAGIC

Each of these visitors to Camelot had a magical connection with one of the creatures in the list below. Choose your answers from the animals given.

toad

snake

dragon

raven

unicorn

Bastet   Unicorn   Pig   Griffin
Beetle   Toad   Lizard   Raven
Serket   Dragon   Cat   Snake

LADY CATRINA

Lady Catrina's beauty was only skin deep. Underneath that elegant façade, there lay a stinking troll who feasted on rotten fruit and slept in a putrid nest. She used her cunning magic to transform herself into an aristocrat and work her way into the heart of Camelot and Uther.

ALVARR

One of Uther's most dangerous enemies, Alvarr is a ruthless warlock who attempted to steal the powerful Crystal of Neahtid that was locked in Camelot's vaults. Making the most of Morgana's fondness for Mordred, he charmed her into taking the magical artefact and made her bring it to him in the Forest of Chemary.

MORDRED

This young Druid boy has exceptional magic powers and is able to communicate silently with Merlin and Morgana. Though the Druids were always believed to be a peaceful race, the Great Dragon has warned that Mordred may one day kill Arthur; it is Merlin's responsibility to stop him.

THE LADY OF THE LAKE

It was a wild, wet night when the cart was driven into Camelot – the cart with the cage on its back. Merlin was shocked when he saw it, because inside the cage was a girl. She was shivering with fear or cold, her clothes were torn and her face was dirty, but Merlin thought she was lovely. Gaius explained that she must have fallen prey to a bounty hunter.

'She's only a girl!' Merlin protested.

'She'll still fetch a good price,' Gaius said. 'Uther offers a handsome reward for anyone with magic.'

Magic! Perhaps that was why Merlin felt drawn towards the girl. She had magic, just like him. But unlike him, she had been found out.

Gaius warned Merlin not to get involved – bounty hunters were dangerous. But Merlin couldn't get the girl's scared, beautiful face out of his mind. He crept out later and used his magic to open the cage. She shrank away as he moved towards her, but he reassured her as best he could while freeing her from her chains. As they crept away, the bounty hunter came round the corner and spotted the empty cage. Quickly, Merlin cast a spell and a tavern sign fell, knocking the man to the ground. Merlin and the girl ran.

He led her into a tunnel deep under the castle. 'He won't find you here,' Merlin said reassuringly.

The girl still seemed scared and wary. 'Why did you help me?' she asked.

Merlin shrugged. She had seen him cast magic; he had no secrets from her. 'It could have been me in that cage,' he said, and at this she seemed to let her guard down a little. She revealed that her name was Freya, and gave a small smile. Pleased, Merlin promised he would return in the morning.

The next day, Halig the bounty hunter had a meeting with King Uther. Gaius listened in alarm as Halig explained that his captive Druid girl had escaped – and two figures had been seen running away. But that wasn't what worried Gaius the most. Halig told the king that the girl was cursed. She was so dangerous that even the Druids were frightened of her . . .

Unaware of these revelations, Merlin hurried down to the cellar. Freya leaped eagerly on the meat and cheese he brought her – food stolen from Prince Arthur's breakfast table.

'Does anyone know you have magic?' she asked him.

He shook his head. 'Only you. And one other person – but I'm not sure he understands.'

'I wish I was like everyone else,' said Freya. 'But . . .'

Merlin completed the sentence. 'You always know deep down you're not.'

For a moment, they looked at each other with understanding. Then Freya turned away. 'Because I'm cursed,' she said.

Merlin couldn't bear that she thought of herself in such a way. 'Magic doesn't have to be a curse. It can be a gift,' he said.

But he wasn't sure if Freya believed him.

Freya told him about her home. It was next to a lake, surrounded by tall mountains. 'In summer there were wild flowers, it was like heaven,' she said.

'Sounds perfect,' said Merlin.

'It was,' Freya told him. 'But then my family died. I've been on my own ever since.'

'You're not on your own any more,' Merlin said. 'I'm going to look after you.'

That night, Merlin dreamed of Freya. He woke up smiling. But Gaius had terrible news – there had been a deadly attack during the night, two people slain by an unknown beast. It worried Merlin, of course it did, but somehow his thoughts kept drifting back to Freya and the smile returned to his face.

As soon as he could, he slipped down to the tunnels to see her. She seemed upset, and he conjured a rose to cheer her up. 'Why are you so good to me?' she said.

'With you, I can just be who I am,' he told her. 'We don't have to hide anything.'

'Merlin, please, listen to me, I'm not like you—' Freya began. But he never found out what she was going to say. They jumped up in alarm as heavy footsteps approached. It was Halig and his men.

Freya was terrified. Eventually, to their relief, the men moved away without discovering them, but the girl couldn't stop crying. 'I can't go back in that cage!' she told Merlin.

'I won't let that happen,' he said. 'I promised I'd look after you and I will. No matter what.' And he leaned forward and kissed her.

Freya kissed him back.

The smile didn't leave Merlin's face for the rest of the day. Even Gaius noticed how happy he seemed.

Merlin had made a decision. A huge decision. But it felt so right! Freya had to leave Camelot: she couldn't stay in the tunnels for ever. But he'd never felt so happy as when he was with her – so he would go too! They would make a home for themselves far away from the city. He'd find a place with mountains and wild flowers and a lake.

His destiny didn't matter. Arthur would be fine without him. All that mattered was that this lovely girl needed him – and he could be happy with her. He could be himself.

That night the beast was back. It killed again. 'The men who saw it spoke of a huge black cat with wings,' Arthur told Uther and Gaius. But there were only human footsteps by the bodies.

The next day, Merlin readied himself for their departure, fetching food and water, horses and blankets. They wouldn't need anything else – all they needed was each other.

He was gathering supplies in Gaius' chambers when the physician came in. He told Merlin that the beast had struck again. 'Ancient chronicles speak of a curse that dooms its victim to turn at the stroke of midnight into a vicious and bloodthirsty beast called a Bastet,' he said. 'And Halig said the Druid girl is cursed. The creature and the girl are one and the same.'

'You're wrong,' Merlin said. 'Freya is just a girl.' But he felt sick inside.

Gaius headed for the door. 'I'm going to tell Uther. I can't let more innocent people die.'

Merlin ran off. He had to warn Freya! But when he reached her alcove in the tunnels, it was empty. She had gone.

He headed back to his room, desperately unhappy. All he hoped was that she was safe. Whatever she might have done, he knew she was a good person. She didn't deserve to die at Uther's hands.

He was lying in his bed, not sleeping, when the warning bell sounded. Freya must have been spotted! Merlin ran outside. Yes, there were Arthur and his knights, and with them the bounty hunter Halig – all advancing on the terrified girl. 'No one escapes from me,' said Halig, but at that moment the clock chimed midnight . . .

In horror, everyone watched the terrible transformation take place. Where the girl had been, there now crouched a giant monster – a great, winged, black cat that pounced on Halig. The men scattered, all except Arthur. The prince lunged at the Bastet, wounding it, and the creature fled. Merlin found the wounded cat. It was a monster, a beast, a creature of nightmare – but it was Freya. He couldn't let them kill it – kill *her*. As Arthur and his men moved in for the kill, Merlin used his magic to send a gargoyle toppling from the castle roof to distract them. The hurt animal managed to fly away.

Merlin found the girl back down in the tunnels. She was curled up in a corner, crying. 'You must hate me,' she said.

'No,' Merlin told her, and he meant it.

'There was a man – he attacked me. I didn't mean to hurt him, but I thought he was going to kill me. But his mother was a sorceress. She said I'd killed her son, and cursed me to kill for ever more.'

Merlin held
her tight. He
knew she was
dying from
her wounds.
But he couldn't leave her to die alone in the darkness.

Merlin carried Freya to a lake. It was surrounded by mountains, and there were wild flowers.

He'd been there before, when he'd had to throw away a magical sword. But Freya was much more difficult to let go. 'There must be something I can do – some way to save you,' he said.

'You've already saved me,' she told him. 'You made me feel loved. One day I will repay you – I promise.' Then she was gone.

Later, the grieving warlock watched the boat carrying Freya float out on to the sunlit waters. With a spell, he brought forth a fire to consume the vessel.

Freya was gone – but he would never forget her.

CREATURES OF MAGIC

The cat-like Bastet was one of several legendary beasts that terrorized Camelot at one time or another. Look at these picture clues and write each character's name in the right place on the grid and the white squares will reveal a ferocious creature once defeated by Merlin's magic.

1. m o r g a n a

2. l a d y c a t r i n a

3. m e r l i n

4. [ ] [ ] [ ] [ ] [ ] [ ] [ ] f

5. f r e y a

6. c e d r i c o s s i a n

7. g w e n

SINISTER SPELLS

Freya's curse was not the only spell to cause havoc in Camelot.
Choose from the words below to complete the sentences on other
dark magic that has affected Uther's kingdom.

Jester	Gargoyles
Afanc	Questing
Knights	Unicorn
Dragonlord	Snakes

1. Arthur came close to death when he was bitten by a magical .... Beast.

2. Cornelius Sigan used a powerful spell to bring the castle's .... to life.

3. Camelot was cursed with food and water shortages after Arthur killed a ....

4. The seven .... of Medhir were lifeless for more than three hundred years, before Morgause's spell revived them.

5. Nimueh the witch sent an .... into the water supply to spread a magical plague across Camelot.

6. The only person with the magical power to control a dragon was a ....

7. Knight Valiant had an enchanted shield embossed with .... that could come to life during battle.

8. King Alined sent his .... to put a love spell on Arthur.

MAGIC POLISH

Arthur has ordered Merlin to clean all these silver goblets. The young warlock has used his magic to get the job done, but one of the goblets has been damaged in the process. Can you spot which one Merlin needs to put right before Arthur gets back?

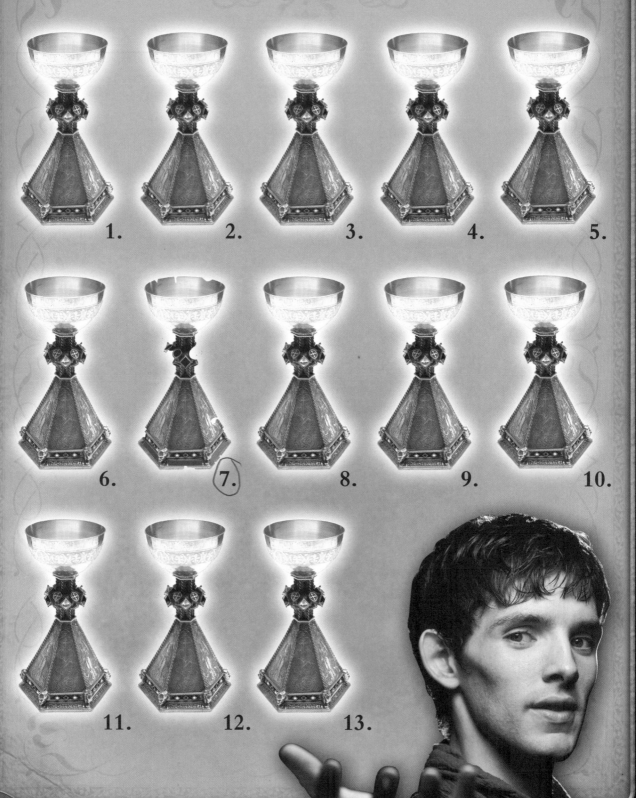

1.   2.   3.   4.   5.

6.   (7.)   8.   9.   10.

11.   12.   13.

HENGIST

❖

This ruthless bandit leader lived on the Mercian border in a crumbling castle and kept a pair of vicious Wilddeoren to dispose of any unwanted guests. His bungled kidnap attempt on Morgana meant he held Gwen for ransom instead, which caused Merlin and Arthur to embark on a secret rescue mission.

MORGAUSE

❖

Morgause is a warrior with fighting skills that match those of any Knight of Camelot, even Arthur. It was Gaius who discovered that she is Morgana's half-sister, whom he smuggled out of Camelot as a baby. She is now a powerful sorceress who used magic in an attempt to destroy the Pendragons and their kingdom.

KING ALINED

❖

Whilst in Camelot for the signing of a peace treaty, this ruthless king instead planned to stir up hostilities between the kingdoms. With the help of his jester's magic powers, he goaded King Olaf into challenging Arthur to a battle – it was sure to end in a declaration of war, whoever won.

EVIL EYES

These eyes belong to enemies of Camelot.
Can you tell who each villain is?

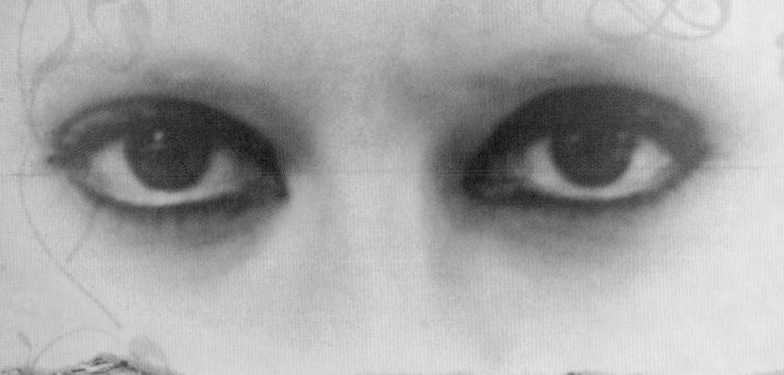

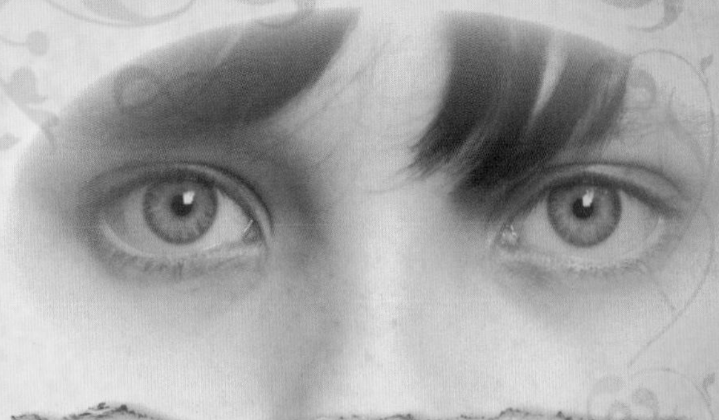

1. <u>MORGAUSE</u>

2. <u>MORDRED</u>

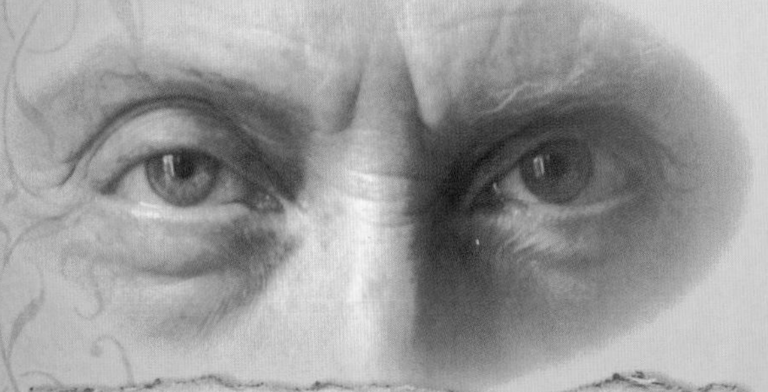

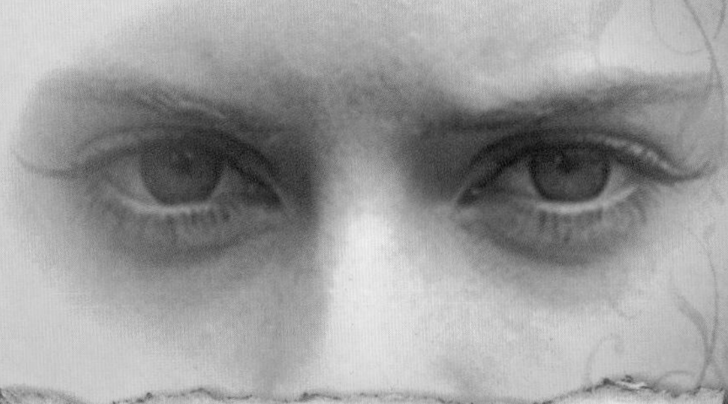

3. <u>aredian</u>

4. <u>NIMEUH</u>

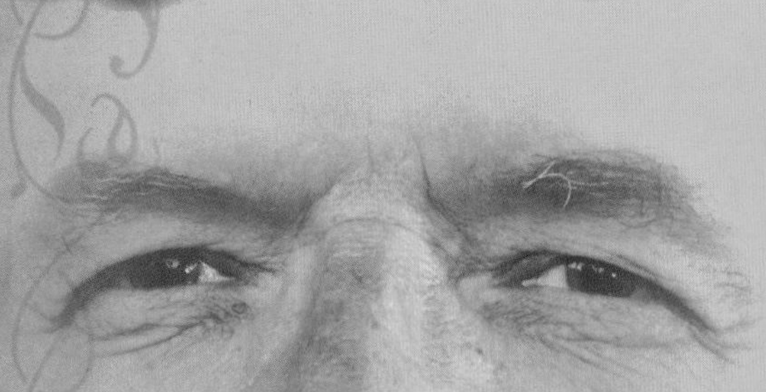

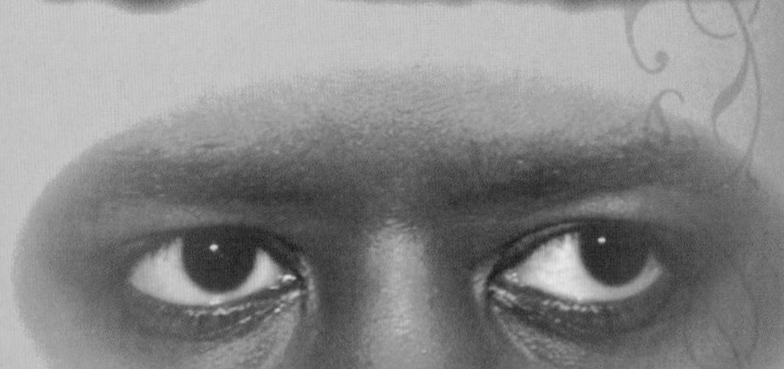

5. <u>KING ALINED</u>

6. _____ ?

ANSWERS

Page 8 – WIZARD WORDSEARCH **Page 9 – MISSING MORGANA** **Page 44 – WITCHFINDER WORDS**

Page 32 – MYSTERY MAN

Page 56 – CREATURES OF MAGIC

Page 18 – TRUTH BE TOLD
1. False – it was a boar. 2. False – it was Cedric.
3. True. 4. False – it was blue. 5. True.
6. False – he used magic. 7. True. 8. True. 9. False.
10. False – Merlin trapped it back in the jewel.

Page 20 – TOMB TREASURE
Row 1 – 12, 15, 18. Row 2 – 8, 16, 32.
Row 3 – 17, 21, 25. Row 4 – 7, 4, 1.
Row 5 – 16, 20, 24. Row 6 – 23, 30, 37.

Page 21 – THE CURSE OF CORNELIUS
Choose from: is, us, on, or, in, lie, sun, run, one, urn,
ore, nor, sir, ice, use, our, lion, lone, sole, lose, line, lens,
sure, sore, sour, soul, cone, core, slur, lice, rice, nice,
rose, nose, rule, role, isle, corn, loser, liner, snore, scone,
score, slice, louse, scour, scorn, ulcer, course, source.

Page 22/3 – MASTERS OF MAGIC
Answers at the bottom of page 23.

Page 33 – DEADLY ASSASSINS
1. King Olaf 2. Mary Collins 3. Lady Catrina
4. Kanan 5. Great Dragon 6. Knight Valiant

Page 45 – HOCUS POTIONS
1. Wolfsbane 2. Hemlock 3. Mandrake 4. Mugwort

Page 46 – ANIMAL MAGIC
Aredian – toad; Valiant – snake; Balinor – Dragon;
Sigan – raven; Lancelot – Griffin; Anhora – Unicorn.

Page 57 – SINISTER SPELLS
1. Questing 2. Gargoyles 3. Unicorn 4. Knights
5. Afanc 6. Dragonlord 7. Snakes 8. Jester

Page 58 – MAGIC POLISH
Goblet no. 7 needs to be put right.

Page 60 – EVIL EYES
1. Morgause 2. Mordred 3. Aredian
4. Nimueh 5. King Alined 6. Myror